GEBOOR

Spiritual Fiction

NANIMA SERIES
BOOK II

DONNA GODDARD

Published by Donna Goddard

Victoria, Australia

Paperback ISBN: 978-0645875577

Large Print ISBN: 978-0645875591

Cover design by Donna Goddard

www.donnagoddard.com

CONTENTS

DISCOVERING GEBOOR

FOR A MOMENT

GOING TO GEBOOR

THREAD OF GEBOOR

PART III
IDOLS
WINTER

WEAVING DREAMS

BEYOND THE SOLSTICE

THE MAN WHO KEPT
HIS DOORS OPEN

TALKING TO THE MOON

PART IV
JOY
SPRING

CHANGING STATES

HEART CENTRE

COSY AND CONSCIOUS

PART I
HEATING UP
SUMMER

SHOPHOUSE

CHAPTER 1

SPECTRUM

"I think you are on the spectrum, boo," said Luna.

Maliyan laughed and thought, *Always the joker.*

Luna wasn't smiling and continued sympathetically, "Lots of people are. I mean, I like people on the spectrum. I find them interesting."

Maliyan wasn't sure what was worse—Luna's diagnosis of her mental state or his trying to make it better by kindly reassuring her that, regardless, it was fine with him. It made it all the funnier or all the more disturbing.

Being in the middle of making a sandwich, he didn't look up but said, "That's why you don't get jokes. You take things literally. Your brain is wired differently."

He had a point—about jokes and her mental wiring. However, Maliyan felt it was more of an unwillingness to go along with conventional thought and conversation patterns rather than an inability to.

Not knowing what to say to Luna's latest announcement, she screwed up her nose, patted Iggy on the head, left Luna to his sandwich, and went to her bedroom.

CHAPTER 2

BEDROOM

I t wasn't exactly a bedroom. It was more of a verandah that had been covered in a makeshift way at some stage in the shop's history. Luna's "house" was two rooms at the back of the shop. One was his bedroom. The other was the kitchen, lounge, and dining room rolled into one. It suited Luna and Iggy perfectly.

When Luna moved to Nanima, it was a lifestyle change more than a business decision. He didn't want to invest in a proper house as he wasn't sure if the cafe would sink or swim.

Maliyan had been living in the shophouse since late spring when Euroka returned from Uluru and took back his hut. After some teething problems, she, Luna, and Iggy adjusted to each other's fairly constant company in a small space.

At first, Maliyan thought that Luna suggested she move in because Euroka was back and her house was rented until the end of summer. However, after a while, she suspected that he had other motives.

Sometimes, she thought it was because he felt she was

strange enough without getting more so down on the Bell all by herself. This morning's conversation about her mental state seemed to support that hypothesis. Sometimes, she wondered if he just wanted her in the shophouse and found a reason to justify asking her. Either way, it was sweet.

Luna was one of the few people Maliyan could tolerate in such close proximity. She assumed that he must have felt the same or, given his nature, he certainly would not have suggested the move. Regardless, summer was moving along, and so was her stay.

CHAPTER 3

ELEMENTAL

Fortunately, the summer had been relatively mild so far. Otherwise, the verandah bedroom would have been a hothouse. Maliyan remembered sleeping in her grandmother's veranda bed in Yan Yan Gurt, the tiny town twenty minutes out of Nanima, where Maliyan's family came from. Although the farmhouse had plenty of bedrooms, her grandmother liked to sleep outside on the verandah. It had mosquito netting nailed to the verandah roof, but it was so old that it was useless.

Maliyan would watch the glowing mass of stars from the bed as a young child. The biting winter air was cold, and the oppressive summer heat was hot, but one got used to it. In retrospect, Maliyan felt that her grandmother's sleeping habits contributed significantly to her longevity and health.

In the yogic tradition, such things are referred to as Bhuta Shuddhi. The words translate as cleansing of the five elements. Our bodies are made of water, earth, wind, fire, and ether (emptiness). If the elements are organised and managed well, there will be health and balance. The body will not complain and will be a valuable tool for the hopefully hundred years we are here.

Element cleansing happens naturally when the body is connected with nature. When people are divorced from nature, particularly in high-rise buildings with climate-controlled artificial environments, they lose touch with their bodies. As a result, they become weak and prone to many illnesses and afflictions.

Most people do not put much effort into properly maintaining their bodies, but the body is the first and most elemental aspect of life to manage and master. Mastery of the physical elements leads to mastery of the mental and energetic elements.

CHAPTER 4

THE DARK

Although Maliyan loved sleeping in her grandmother's verandah bed, she loved it only when her grandmother was in it. Naturally, the grandmother went to sleep much later than her, so Maliyan had to go out on the veranda alone.

It was very dark.

Most children have some fear of the dark, but Maliyan was intensely afraid of it. And she was afraid of it for much longer than a child usually is. She was well into her teen years before the fear lessened. Even then, it was still significant.

She saw things in the dark, and they weren't good. Usually, it was some manner of black flying thing that wished harm to her and anyone else it came into contact with. Most of it would have been imagined, but maybe not all, as she was both extra-sensitive and extra-sensory.

She couldn't tell anyone about it. It would have been too embarrassing to say that she was terrified of the dark, particularly to farmers who are tough and brave and walk around in the dark all the time. Anyway, no one would have known what to say other than, "Don't be silly. It's not real. Go to bed." And that wouldn't have helped.

In the end, her fear of the dark outweighed her love of sleeping with her grandmother. So, she told her grandmother she wanted to sleep in the house. Her grandmother looked confused and sad but never asked why. She would have assumed that Maliyan had simply outgrown the enjoyment of sleeping with her. The sad look in her grandmother's eyes was still imprinted on Maliyan's consciousness.

LET ME IN

CHAPTER 5

LAURA-BELLA

Early on in Maliyan's stay in Euroka's hut, a woman knocked on her door.

"Hello," said the woman in a surprised but friendly manner. "I'm Laura-Bella, an artist friend of Euroka. Is he out?"

Once she explained where Euroka was, Maliyan invited her in because the woman didn't appear to want to go. She seemed to sense what Euroka might be doing. Anyway, Maliyan liked her. Laura-Bella looked around the hut carefully, paying particular attention to the didgeridoo on the bed.

After that day, she often called in to ask Maliyan if she wanted to join her on her morning walk along the Bell. Intelligent, creative, and emotionally available, she made a natural and interesting female friend for Maliyan. However, it wasn't her intelligence, creativity, or emotional availability that was the deciding factor in her friendship with Maliyan.

It was pain.

Not the sort of pain that generally accompanies

humans from birth to grave (with only minor variations), but the pain that accompanies a serious student of life. It was the sort of pain that pushes one to let go of the known and reach for something else. It was the sort of pain that makes growth inescapable, irresistible, and irreversible.

CHAPTER 6

BELL-BELL

B*ack to now:*
        After their morning excursion along the Bell, Laura-Bella and Maliyan wound their way to Luna Tiks.

With plaintive eyes, Laura-Bella suddenly said, "Let me in."

Maliyan's usually sweet composure turned into a much more intense one. She did not need to ask what Laura-Bella meant. Nor did she want to waste time by objecting that she was already *in*.

"Yes, with this condition," said Maliyan with unflinching eyes.

She waited for Laura-Bella's entire sharpened focus—a focus drawn from lifetimes previous as much as current.

"You must entirely accept the relationships in my life," said Maliyan, "and the form they take, including yours with me."

Being a passionate and whole-hearted person, Laura-Bella immediately opened her mouth to accept.

However, Maliyan stopped her and said, "No, think on

it a while. Once you accept, if you later wish to withdraw your acceptance, you will suffer deeply."

A touch of panic crept into Laura-Bella's eyes.

Maliyan softened her demeanour and said, "I would never hurt you. I could not hurt you, but it's the nature of the beast."

She glanced through the shop window and saw that Luna was watching them intently.

"The same is true for us all," said Maliyan. "If we taste the fruit ahead and then reroute, we will never again be satisfied with anything less than what we reached for with our higher self."

ONE WEEK LATER, AT THE BELL:

"I have made my decision," said Laura-Bella with the conviction of a soldier ready to risk all in the battle.

Maliyan didn't ask what her decision was. Instead, she bent down and took some earth from the banks of the Bell. Mixing it into a paste with the river's water, she put it on her thumb and drew a line down Laura-Bella's forehead.

"I name you Bell-Bell," said Maliyan. "You run with this river."

CHAPTER 7

WAY OUT

L*ater that morning, in Luna Tiks:*
"You have dirt on your face," Luna said to Bell-Bell.

She laughed but didn't wipe it off. After she left, Luna recalled her and Maliyan's conversation outside the shop window a week ago.

"What do you two talk about that's so serious?" he asked Maliyan.

Seriousness wasn't a major feature of Luna and Maliyan's relationship. Nor was it the way to reach Luna. He was a feeler, much more than a thinker. He was loved and hurt, won and lost, helped and hindered, healed and harmed by virtue of the heart.

He hated conflict and did not deal with it well. Luna and Maliyan's relationship had its inevitable ups and downs, closeness and distance, but they didn't fight. On the rare occasions that Maliyan got mad at him, he was so badly affected that she quickly regretted it. He was not robust in that way. Emotional stress could really throw him.

Maliyan felt that, with time, he would become less prone to such delicacies, but for now, she made it her business not to stress him unless it was essential. Regardless, that did not eliminate all the stress he did to himself.

At that moment, the building owner of the dance school across the road came in and ordered his usual coffee.

"Got anyone interested in taking over the dance school lease yet?" asked Luna.

"No, mate," said the man.

Although he called Luna his mate, he wasn't really a mate to anyone, and Luna neither liked nor trusted him. But, he was business. Luna sometimes joked to Maliyan that he was as bad as the guy, "Both selling our souls for business."

"Do you think we could offer him free coffee in exchange for me practising in the dance studio while it's unoccupied?" Maliyan asked Luna.

Luna said, "There's no *we* in the coffee. It's mine."

Nevertheless, a few hours later, he passed Maliyan a key and said, "His words were, 'You can use it, but if anything happens to the studio, it's on your head, and it will cost you much more than coffee.'"

As the heat of the day quietened its burn, Luna returned to his morning question and said, "I was being serious. I want to know what you and Laura-Bella talk about. Let me in. "

Maliyan sighed slightly and started to brightly relay some of the things that Bell-Bell liked to talk about. Within two minutes, Luna had lost all interest.

"Okay," he said with glazed eyes. "That's enough *in*. I'm going *out*. Out to walk Iggy."

At the mention of his name, Iggy appeared by Luna's side. Luna touched him adoringly, turned his gaze to Maliyan, wrapped his arm around her, and kissed the top of her head.

"Love you," he said on the way out.

SORRY, NOT SORRY

CHAPTER 8

SORRY

As the electricity at the dance school was disconnected, Maliyan had to use the studio when it wasn't too hot or too dark. The morning shafts of light filtered through the high windows, spotlighting all the airborne dust. Dust on the wooden floor made it slippery for felt-soled dance shoes, so she ran a wet mop over it. It became her warm-up. Up and down, she systematically followed the timber lines in time with samba music from her phone.

Samba is a party dance, so it has lots of energy. As Maliyan didn't like parties, she thought of samba as earthy and tribal. It worked just as well in getting her body into gear.

Maliyan realised that a ringing sound was not coming from the loud samba beat but from her phone.

"Hi, Rex," she said. "Strange you should ring now as I'm in the dance studio across the road from home."

Rex (Maliyan's ex-dance partner) was about to ask *what home,* but changed his mind.

"Emma has been ill," said Rex.

Emma was his wife.

"I'm sorry to hear that," said Maliyan.

"It's okay," said Rex. "She's getting better now."

Maliyan waited for him to continue.

"In the process of trying to get her well," said Rex, "we went to a healer."

That's odd, thought Maliyan. *Failure is a great incentive to seek alternatives.*

Trying to find the words for something he didn't understand, Rex hesitated. If we can explain something easily, it's because we understand it. We struggle to explain when we don't know what is important and what is not.

Maliyan remembered trying to explain to Rex about dance lectures and classes she had been to without him. As the concepts were new to her at that time, it would come out as a great jumble of information or as a blank. He would be none the wiser about what was actually said in the lecture or done in the class.

"Yes?" said Maliyan expectantly.

"You know how I can sometimes get," said Rex, "um... sort of..."

"Mean?" offered Maliyan.

"No, not mean," said Rex indignantly.

"Oh, right, no. Not mean," said Maliyan, who was sorry, not sorry.

If he keeps being this offended, thought Maliyan, *he's never going to get anywhere.*

"I know that I can be a little arrogant," said Rex, "but I'm not mean."

In Rex's mind, arrogance was a forgivable sign of confidence. He did not understand that arrogance makes people unteachable. Nor did he understand that arrogance comes from fear—fear of not knowing, of being stupid, of being wrong. Arrogance is a protection, a faulty one. There's no point in making arrogant people feel more insecure.

"Anyway," said Rex, "the healer said that I sometimes spiral into a dark place because of what happened to me when I was born."

"Really?" said Maliyan, who already knew this.

Although the healer's words did not surprise Maliyan, recalling her dream from the night before brought an unexpected sense of recognition. She had been holding a newborn, desperately rocking back and forth and sobbing. When she woke, she assumed it belonged to someone else — someone else's baby, someone else's trauma — but she didn't know who.

"Isn't that strange?" said Rex. "Of course, I can't remember any of that stuff, and it all worked out fine, but the healer said that abandonment at birth becomes a deep-seated trauma. I asked her what to do about it. She said it would gradually heal if I learned not to react to situations and tried to understand my fears."

The studio was heating up. Maliyan was sweating, even though she was standing still.

"Thanks for telling me," she said as Rex hung up the phone.

CHAPTER 9

NOT SORRY

"What are you thinking about?" asked Luna as Maliyan stared into thin air that evening.

"I'm thinking about the story of Krishna and Radha," said Maliyan. "Do you want to know why Krishna never married Radha even though she was the love of his life?"

Luna knew that whether he wanted to know or not, he was about to find out.

"Why don't you tell me?" he said.

"Krishna first saw Radha when he was seven, and she was twelve," said Maliyan. "They instantly fell in love. It is said that when Radha first laid eyes on Krishna, he became part of her eyes. From then on, she always carried him inside herself. As children, they lived in different villages and could not often see each other. Krishna's desires were very powerful, and, as it turned out, his whole village had to relocate close to Radha's village."

Luna shuffled restlessly on the lounge.

"Even though Krishna loved Radha very much, he did not marry her," continued Maliyan. "After nine years together, he left the village when he turned sixteen. In time, he married eight other women (which was the custom), and Radha's mother also arranged for her to marry. Nevertheless, Radha and Krishna's lifelong love for each other became a symbol of eternal devotion. When one is spoken of, the other is never far away."

Luna looked like he wasn't sure if that was supposed to be an inspiration or a tragedy, a romance or a horror. His expression made Maliyan laugh.

❦

LATER THAT NIGHT, MALIYAN LAY IN BED, LISTENING TO the mounting storm and thinking about Krishna becoming part of Radha's eyes. She threw the covers off and felt her way through the dark to the other side of the verandah, where a dripping noise was getting more persistent.

Suddenly, a loud crash shook the whole house, and water sprayed everywhere. Maliyan found herself on the floor. She wasn't sure if the force pushed her over or if she had instinctively dropped for cover. The light turned on in the front of the house, and Luna came rushing into the verandah bedroom.

"Are you alright?" he called. "Maliyan, are you alright?"

He saw a white figure at the end of the room.

"I'm alright," said the ghostly figure, trying to wipe the white powder off her face.

Right above Maliyan's bed, the roof had collapsed. The bedroom was a mess of broken wood, plaster, and water. They rescued what they could, pushed the bed to one side, and placed a large tub under the leak.

"We can't do anything else till morning," said Luna. "Sleep with me."

After a shower, Maliyan went to Luna's room. Iggy lifted his head, cocked it to one side, and then lay back down on the mat with one eye open and one eye closed.

Once Maliyan climbed into Luna's bed, he put his hand on her now-clean face and said, "I thought you were dead."

Then, he pulled her body next to his and became part of Maliyan's eyes.

❦

THE NEXT MORNING, LUNA AND MALIYAN STARED AT the wet mess in the verandah bedroom.

"I'm sorry about the ceiling," said Maliyan.

"I'm not," said Luna.

NOT FUNNY

CHAPTER 10

BELLY UP

Valentine's Day had come and gone. Summer had come and almost gone. Maliyan's stay in the shophouse had definitely gone.

It all started with a stomachache gone wrong. Luna said he had a bellyache. He said it was because he ate too much. Maliyan said it wasn't. He *had* eaten too much, but that was the least of his problems. The real problem was obvious—obvious to Maliyan but not to Luna.

A week after the occasion of the collapsed ceiling and collapsed boundaries between the two of them, Luna started spiralling into the dark territory of unconsciousness, where all sorts of irrational, hurtful, and destructive things come dancing out of the closet. He knew he was spiralling but couldn't stop it. Or wouldn't.

One evening, he said caustically, "There's a reason I live alone."

The toxicity was directed at himself as much as Maliyan.

"Stop," said Maliyan. "You don't have to do this. It's a

reaction to things you are avoiding in your mind. Just look at the darn things. They won't kill you."

No doubt, Luna thought there was a higher probability that the thoughts *would* kill him than there was of Maliyan being right. He got worse and worse until even his ability to be funny abandoned him.

On that far-from-funny note, Maliyan returned to her house the day the renters vacated it.

CHAPTER 11

THIS WILL PASS

It's best to let oneself cry when one is sad. The tears sting, but they are finite in number. Cry them out, and they'll run out. If you never learn to cry properly, then you can't get the hurt out. The tears tell you how long to cry. It's nothing to do with what you decide. They tell *you*—they tell you everything. They tell you if something is worth crying about in the first place. They tell you how sad it is. They tell you how deep it is.

Maliyan knew that Luna would be hurting, too. How could he not be? For something to hurt when it dismantles, it has to have been made into enough of a thing that it's painful to pull apart.

When it came to pulling apart, Maliyan knew what helped.

First, tell yourself *this, too, will pass*. It will.

Then, *remember the good things*. When hurting, it is easy to gravitate towards the bad and forget the million good things, big and small, that someone gave us. The bond was built on the good, not the bad. If it is a strong bond, a bond worth crying about, then there must have been lots of good. Remembering it puts things into perspective. It reminds us that people, relationships, and life have their ups and downs, their coming togethers and their pulling apart.

There are eight billion people in the world. Half of them are the opposite sex (which suits most people). That's a big pool to pull from. If someone doesn't want you, or wants someone else, or doesn't want anyone, or doesn't know what they want, then there are other people who will want you in their life in some viable, respectable, reciprocal way. That doesn't mean jumping from person to person with every passing problem. Nor does it mean devaluing the enormous gift of cherished, destined relationships. However, it does mean that we don't beg like a pauper. No one wants a beggar. If we feel bright and hopeful about our future, we will tend to let our loved ones be as they wish—whether that includes us or not. It takes away the desperation. It lessens the grief. It builds the foundation for forgiveness.

Understanding dissolves anger. Many destructive things that people do are not primarily intended to hurt their loved ones. It's often that the person doesn't know what else to do. Their emotional development hits a roadblock, and they detour into their mental programming. They would not do it if they knew a better way. No one suffers on purpose. And no one would create suffering for others if they knew how to live in a way that did not cause emotional pain and create karma.

Pain is the price you pay for another's heart. No matter who causes the heartbreak, it will affect all involved. Breaking hearts hurt. If you're not up for the ride, then don't get involved. Before giving your heart to another, you should ask yourself whether the person is worth a broken heart because the breaking will surely happen sooner or later.

And that, too, will pass.

PART II
SACRED SPACES
AUTUMN

POUSTINIA

CHAPTER 12

POUSTINIK DANCER

Something about the dance studio this morning reminded Maliyan of a poustinia. Its lack of people, furniture, and electricity. Its striking emptiness.

Poustinia is a Russian word for a sparsely furnished cabin where one goes to pray and fast. Its most fundamental element is its aloneness. Alone, except for God. In Russia, poustiniks often live on the edges of towns and are available to their communities for spiritual help.

Although Maliyan had plenty of self-starting drive to dance in her poustinia, there was no doubt that another body, another being, another type of energy gave dance a different and wonderful dimension.

I don't mind being a poustinik dancer, she thought, *but I danced so much better when Rex danced with me.*

The energy of a healthy, fully functioning male is so different to feminine energy. It pushed her and activated her as a female dancer. His dancing body turned on a switch in her body marked "move" (preferably in time with the music).

We need our men to dance, thought Maliyan. *If we want them to dance, we have to seduce them. But with what?*

A young visiting teacher once told her, "Be sexier. A woman's assets are her hair, boobs, and butt."

Maliyan laughed because she thought he was joking. Surely, it was a joke. It wasn't.

She looked in the mirror at her hair (no longer than a boy's) and her boobs and butt, which were... ordinary as far as she could tell. She turned towards the teacher and then to his dance partner, who was practising in the far corner of the studio. She was definitely all hair, boobs, and butt—big and luscious. However, she was neither big nor luscious when it came to depth and heart.

Although Maliyan understood his focus, she knew that even with ten more years, hair, boobs, and butt would no longer cut it as inspiration. By thirty, experienced male dancers have seen enough hair, boobs, and butt to last a lifetime. Besides, a significant proportion of male dancers are gay. Female hair, boobs, and butt don't pull much weight.

If we want our men to dance, thought Maliyan, *we have to inspire them. Not with blatant sexuality. That is too common, too little. But with something more, something bigger, something that will give them a reason to want to dance.*

The greatest joy of partner dancing is difference. You feed off each other and make the other better and more than we can be on our own. We need difference to help us grow and blossom. It is what happens in life-enhancing relationships. Imagine living with a clone of yourself. How utterly boring. How uninspiring. How intolerable.

We are drawn to people who change us with their difference. Not change us into less of ourselves but into something we cannot be in our own solitary poustinias.

CHAPTER 13

SAINT FRANCIS

A man about Maliyan's age stopped outside the studio and wrestled with his shopping bags and the coffee he bought from Luna Tiks. He was tall and slim with enough grey hair to be proud of. Something about his eyes looked very familiar. They were soft and kind, introspective and pious.

"Francis?" asked Maliyan as she quickly went outside to greet him. "Saint Francis? Is that you?"

Hearing his nickname from three decades ago, he knew the woman could only be one person: his at-one-stage girlfriend.

He laughed, hugged her, and said, "That's a name no one has called me in a long time."

Francis first visited Nanima when he was not long out of school. He belonged to a charismatic community of lay people called *Spirit of Joy* in the city's inner suburbs. At that time, Francis was seriously considering becoming a brother or monk. To get direction, he decided to spend a month in the newly established poustinia outside of

Nanima on the property of one of the community's families.

After a week in the poustinia, he met Maliyan, also fresh out of school. Every day, they kept meeting to talk about the community and the poustinia, which they both found fascinating.

Not only did he not take Catholic order vows, but he decided to take a girlfriend instead. With his help, Maliyan moved to the city into one of the community houses, which was ever so much fun and full of laughter.

After a year, Maliyan ended the relationship by starting another relationship with someone else. That may seem mean (and Francis certainly thought it was), but he quickly found a lovely girl, married her, and proceeded to have half a dozen children to add to the Catholic population. It wasn't that Maliyan wasn't "lovely", but the one he married was more "lovely" for him. Maliyan had too much fire for Francis. Fire, for some people, just burns them. It doesn't ignite them. You want to be switched on, not incinerated.

"We're empty nesters now," explained Francis. "Frankly, I'm tired."

"You've been flat out for the last thirty years," said Maliyan.

She didn't say (but Francis knew she meant), *And for a person like you, who has such a high propensity for contemplation, being in the world has taken its toll.*

"I remembered the poustinia," said Francis, "and asked if it was still operating. The family said no one had been in it for many years, but they would dearly love for someone to go there and use it for what it was intended. I'm not sure what state it will be in."

He laughed in his good-natured, somewhat serious way

and said, "It'll probably be in about the same state as I feel. So, we will meet each other on equal terms."

Maliyan thought that the poustinia was never so loved by anyone as it was by Francis and that, really, it was his poustinia all along.

Looking guiltily at his coffee, Francis confessed, "I'm supposed to be fasting."

Maliyan shrugged and asked, "How long have you got?"

"As long as I need," said Francis. "I have long service leave, and my beautiful wife is giving me the gift of time."

"Do you want to be left alone?" asked Maliyan.

"You can come," said Francis.

"Don't worry," laughed Maliyan. "I promise I won't come every day like last time. When you are ready, let me know, and I'll come out and visit my Saint Francis of Poustinia."

DISCOVERING GEBOOR

CHAPTER 14

PASSOVER

Bell-Bell sat at her favourite spot on the edge of the Bell. It was quite a distance from the town centre. So, it was reserved for days when she felt like a long walk or needed one. Today was the latter. One of her close friends was in the process of passing over. It wasn't only the impending bereavement disturbing Bell-Bell, but the task of being present to a dying person. It's intense.

It was almost Easter. The 8-day Jewish Passover had begun. She couldn't help feeling that by the time Passover was over, her friend's life would be too.

Although Passover is a celebration of escape and freedom, it is smeared with the brush of painful loss. Around 1200 B.C., the Egyptian Pharaoh refused to free the Israelite slaves. As a result, a terrible plague was brought upon the land in which the firstborn son of each family—from king to lowest slave—would be killed. To spare the Israelite families, Moses told them to smear lamb's blood on their doors and that the angel of death would pass them over. Thus, *Passover*.

Trying to shake the collective sorrow of Passover and

the personal sorrow of her friend's situation, she lay back on a large, flat rock and put her bare feet in the cool water. The rock cradled her back with its permanence. She did not know the area had become a sacred Aboriginal site thirty years ago. This was where Maliyan's high school boyfriend died in a flash flood.

He was in his last year of school. Having a part-time job with a neighbouring farmer, he often moved the sheep from paddock to paddock. The river was running low, so he decided that the sheep would be able to get across it rather than taking them the long way. As it hadn't been raining in Nanima, he didn't think twice about the water level. However, many miles upstream, it had been raining heavily. A wall of rumbling water was heading his way.

He was almost to the other side when he heard a roar in the distance. He thought it was the new express train that flew along the tracks with alarming speed, occasionally with fatal consequences for a few hard-of-hearing senior drivers who were used to the railway crossings being a casual affair (not look both ways and cross like a bat out of hell if it's coming).

The boy noticed panic in the sheep's eyes and went back to pick up some of the lambs who had strayed from their mothers. The alarm was growing on all sides. By the time he saw the wall of water, it was too late. He, the lambs, and some of the terrified mothers were swept downstream and drowned.

His family mob made the place a sacred site—a place to connect with him and other dreaming spirits.

CHAPTER 15

ALLELUIA

Not feeling any better, Bell-Bell decided to head home. However, she saw Maliyan's car at a nearby shack and decided to find out what she was doing.

"I hope I'm not interrupting anything," she said somewhat awkwardly when she entered the poustinia and saw Maliyan holding hands with a man she didn't know.

Although Francis was shocked by the unannounced visitor, Maliyan laughed and said, "You're thirty years too late for that."

Francis looked like he thought that was an inappropriate joke for a stranger.

"We have reverted to our old-time Pentecostal type of praying," explained Maliyan.

After a month's stay in the poustinia, this was Francis's last day before returning to the city. He said that the mornings were starting to get a bit nippy. Early autumn was his favourite time to use the poustinia. It had no creature comforts (or even electricity), and the weather up till now was generally favourable with the lingering warmth of summer and none of the bitterness of winter.

Maliyan had been out to see him every week. Although both had long since left their Catholic Charismatic ways behind, they spontaneously started praying together in the ways they once knew and loved. Hands-on healing, giving messages they felt were spiritually inspired, enthusiastically singing the hymns they could remember (sometimes making up the words), waving their hands in the air with shouts of alleluia, and various other things that were fun back then and, somehow, seemed fun again now.

They shared a deep, sincere, and humble love of the Divine. No matter how they prayed, it was going to work.

CHAPTER 16

TIED TO THE MOUNTAIN

Seeing the same hopeful, searching look in Bell-Bell's eyes as when she first came to Euroka's hut, Maliyan suggested, "Come in and join us. This is our last run."

Maliyan smiled fondly at Francis, and he, in turn, kindly said to Bell-Bell, "Yes, come in, please. Do join us. That's what the poustinia is for."

Although Bell-Bell was unfamiliar with the type of prayer, she quickly caught on and threw herself into it with gusto. At the end of the "prayer meeting", they did their usual personal readings.

"I have a message for you that I have been keeping to myself as I wasn't sure if I heard it correctly," Francis said to Maliyan.

With all eyes on him, Francis stood up, went to the wooden table, took a small pile of yellowing cards, and returned to his seat.

"This pile has been here for decades," he said. "It's pictures of various local places with a few words on the back. I assume that everything in the pile is a sacred place."

He showed the cards, one by one: the Nanima Caves, the rivers Bell and Wambul, Mount Arthur (which they could see through the dirty poustinia window), the Aboriginal Mission, and some of the town's churches. Unlike the rest of the cards, the last one didn't have a picture. It had a poem.

Handing it to Maliyan, Francis said, "It's for you. I don't know why, but...."

He hesitated, as he was not prone to false prophesying and then said, "I think you have to go there."

Maliyan took the card and read the poem out loud.

> Everything is stored in
> the fabric of Geboor.
> Take a thread and
> pull it towards you.
> Not any thread.
> If you take the wrong one,
> it will fray away.
>
> Take the thread that is yours.
> Tie it around you.
> See how it remains anchored
> in the bowels of Geboor.
> Wind it around you so
> many times, you forget that
> once it was not a part of you.

When you come down,
the thread will come too.
You will be tied to the mountain.
Make something from it.
Make it into the garment
of your life and you will
breathe your existence with ease.

CHAPTER 17

LYING LADY

"Where is it?" asked Maliyan. "I have never heard of Geboor."

Nor had the other two.

"I don't know about Geboor," said Maliyan, "but I have been dreaming about a mountain that looks like a woman lying down."

The other two were acutely interested and wanted more information.

"The main bit of the mountain is the shape of a well-endowed woman," said Maliyan.

"Big boobs," suggested Bell-Bell.

"It has a pointy bit on the top like a...."

"Nipple," suggested Bell-Bell.

"And it has a protruding part further down like a...."

"Pubic bone," said Bell-Bell.

"And then the legs lazily stretch out over the country-side," said Maliyan. "It's not just the shape of it that has such strong feminine energy. It's the very mountain. It radiates a vast sort of sensuality like...."

"Mother Earth!" said Bell-Bell triumphantly.

"And I know where it is!" she added with equal exhilaration. "My father lives at the foot of such a mountain. When I drive from the city to his home, one hour along the freeway, I see the shape you are describing. It's called Mount Macedon. The locals call it Lady Macedon. At least, a lot of the local men call it that, including my father."

Feeling somewhat left out, Francis said, "Ahh, that's great, but the mountain on the card is not called Mount Macedon or Lady Macedon. It's called Geboor."

"Message your father and ask if the mountain has another name," said Maliyan.

Francis and Maliyan could tell by Bell-Bell's thrilled demeanour that it was the right mountain.

"Its Aboriginal name is Geboor," explained Bell-Bell.

"If it's only an hour from the city," said Maliyan, "then it's probably somewhere near High Community, which I visited in the mountains about this time last year. That's a four-hour drive from here. Not so far, by country standards."

"Oh, no," smiled Bell-Bell. "Not *our* city. Not *our* part of the Great Dividing Range. You have to go all the way to the southern end of the Range to *that* city. It's a full day's drive from Nanima. A long way, even by country standards."

As the three parted company, Bell-Bell noticed how much better she felt. She didn't need to figure out anything about anything. Simply being in the poustinia with the right kind of folk had put things into perspective. It wasn't even necessary to know what that perspective was. The perspective had sorted things out by itself.

And Bell-Bell decided to leave it like that.

FOR A MOMENT

CHAPTER 18

THE KEY

Before Maliyan could go to Geboor, she had to talk
to Luna. She had been into Luna Tiks most mornings for coffee since leaving the shophouse at the
end of summer, but that was merely the exchange of
civility.

After the breakdown of their living arrangement, she
deliberately made herself go to Luna Tiks. If you abruptly
stop seeing someone after a relationship crisis, it can
become so awkward and difficult to see them that you
never do. That creates a lot of bad karma and certainly
works against healing. Even if it's uncomfortable, it's
better to see the person.

Besides, she wanted to see him.

He already knew of her plan to go to Geboor because
of the few sentences they exchanged along the way. This
morning, she told him she would return the dance studio
key as she didn't know how long she would be away. As she
hoped to talk to him properly, she said she would return it
after closing hours.

CHAPTER 19

TOP OF THE LIST

"I've got the morbs," said Luna when Maliyan passed him the key and asked how he was.

Maliyan smiled at the reinvention of the old-fashioned expression about being morbid. It reminded her of the other funny expressions Luna had. He was never boring. In fact, he often blurted out spot-on (but inappropriate) comments about all sorts of things.

She remembered him going through a stage of saying that she was *fickle*. He must have been mad about something or other. Then, when he got over it, he went through a stage of saying she was *fluid*. Fluid was certainly more complimentary than fickle. Often, it wasn't the thing he said but how he said it. Whatever he said, he threw himself into. It carried a certain force—either as a joke, a compliment, an insult, or an insight.

Another meaningful memory came to mind about lipstick. When Maliyan was recovering from her back operation last year, she started wearing lipstick whenever she left the house. She was physically struggling. It was affecting her mental equilibrium and well-being. She must have thought that the lipstick (which she usually reserved for special occasions) would make her more functional. After she wore it for a few days, Luna said, "Don't feel you have to put makeup on for us. We like you just as you are." That was the end of the lipstick.

She leaned on Luna heavily during her recovery period. Every day, she visited the cafe and sat there much longer than usual. At some level, Luna would have sensed her drawing on his life force, health, and vitality, but he didn't stop it. He was generally not tolerant of clinginess.

He once told her that before falling in love with Iggy, he wasn't a fan of dogs. He pretended to other people that he was because, otherwise, they would get upset that he didn't like their dogs. "But, really," he explained, "I thought dogs were too hairy and too needy."

Regardless, Luna let Maliyan lean on him.

And, on Maliyan's list of people, he went to the top.

CHAPTER 20

ALL OF ME

I t's a fucking long way," said Luna as he turned the studio key around in his palm.

He didn't say that going to Geboor was a stupid idea, that it didn't make sense, or that she was crazy. He said it was a long way, which it was.

"When you were here in the shophouse, I felt content," Luna said honestly. "For just a moment, I felt perfectly content."

So why did you destroy it? thought Maliyan.

"Why do you think it took me so long to start a relationship with you?" asked Luna. "And why do you think, after one week, I destroyed it?"

"I don't know," said Maliyan.

"Nearly all my past relationships have been with men," said Luna, "not women."

Maliyan tried to process what that meant and why they hadn't discussed it before. She was certainly aware that he wasn't a macho man, but she saw him as a balanced person (not a queer man). His way of communicating with people, his lack of predatory behaviour towards women, his tolerance towards people who were different, and many of his mannerisms were definitely the sorts of things cultivated in same-sex communities.

She wasn't shocked to find out he had male-male relationships, but she felt it wasn't relevant to *their* relationship. She had always responded to the relationship he offered her, not to what he was or wasn't to other people.

"But I love you," she said.

"I love you too," said Luna.

"So, does it matter then?" she asked.

"It matters to me," said Luna.

"I see," said Maliyan.

"You could stay here in Nanima," suggested Luna, "and accept the situation for what it is."

Maliyan thought for a moment and said, "No, I won't do that. You will want *all* of me, but you will only be willing to give me back part of you."

"Clearly," said Luna, "I won't want *all* of you."

"You will want *all* that really matters," said Maliyan. "You will want all of my heart so that I won't be able to give it to anyone else. And then you will do what you want with your own. No, I'm not willing to do that. Not for you. Not for anyone. And mostly, not for myself."

GOING TO GEBOOR

CHAPTER 21

FOLLOWING THE RANGE

A touch of light hit the Nanima horizon, and Maliyan began the long journey to Geboor. She crisscrossed the countryside towards the Great Dividing Range. As well as watching the colours of the morning sky, she had to watch out for kangaroos. They move quickly and impulsively, with no road sense, and are most active at dawn and dusk. For their sake and hers, an unscheduled meeting was best avoided.

Maliyan told herself that once the beauty of the morning and the danger of the kangaroos had passed, she would settle into something "useful". It didn't happen. Although she intended to use the drive for listening to audiobooks, they remained unopened. Something else, however, did open.

As she followed the Great Dividing Range southward, through farms and little towns, she felt no need to listen to anything or even think about anything. It seemed enough just to be alive, to be the mountain range's travelling companion, and to be part of life. It was silence and aliveness in a pure, still, aware, and awake form. It was more than enough.

Even before she got to Geboor, its thread seemed to be winding itself around her.

CHAPTER 22

BLACK FOREST

The mountain range was on Maliyan's left for most of the journey. She stayed in the pasture-land and stopped here and there but dared not stay too long as she still had far to go before nightfall.

Towards the end of her drive, she moved into the hills of the Macedon Ranges. The greenness, wetness, and cold-ness increased with the climb. The air became dense. It was thick with possibility, both in a material and energetic form. Riddled with the multitudinous forms that multiply in such environments, it was highly fertile for nature and people. The area would suit creatives down to the ground. For a spiritual seeker, it was ideal.

At dusk, Maliyan came to a mist-shrouded town called Black Forest. She pulled up at Bell-Bell's father's house and could see Geboor in the distance, a fifteen-minute drive to the top. Bell-Bell's father was in a nursing home, but did not want to sell his home. The family were glad to have her look after it.

And so, in the charming town of Black Forest, at the

foot of the exquisite Geboor mountain, Maliyan moved into a different time of her life.

THREAD OF GEBOOR

CHAPTER 23

IT IS YOU

It was a few weeks until winter began in earnest, although it already felt cold to Maliyan, who was used to the more northern temperatures. The top of Geboor was clearly not going to be a safe place to drive during the winter months in a little city car. There would be too much black ice on the narrow roads, and you could easily slide off the mountain and become part of it in the wrong sort of way. She drove to the summit most days while she still could. As Francis's poem in the poustinia instructed, she pulled a thread from Geboor or, more to the point, the thread pulled her.

One crisp, clear morning on Geboor, looking down to Black Forest in one direction and the faraway city in the opposite direction, she heard more of the Geboor poem.

Look at the town below.
It is you.
Look at the city in the distance.
It is you.
Every rumbling car, pacing person,
running child, and wagging dog
is you.

Look to the far reaches of the range.
It is you.
Look to the endless sky.
It is you.
And when the heavens are full
of the shining masses of long ago,
know that you, too, were long ago.

A story of old,
still being told.
Like the burned-up stars
giving their fire until
they are no more.
You, too, are that.

CHAPTER 24

HANGING ROCK

Geboor was a powerful place, but it was also round, soft, and feminine. From its summit, you could see, a few kilometres away, a different sort of imposing structure called Hanging Rock. Before it had an English name, it was the intersecting point of three Aboriginal groups and served as a gathering place. Its cliff-like precipices, with seemingly bottomless drops, made Hanging Rock ideal for ceremonies, initiations, conflict resolution, marriages, and trade.

Places, like people, have their own unique energy. Hanging Rock was vibrant, intense, otherworldly, mysterious, changeable, and predominantly masculine. It was a balance to Geboor.

Of the two landmarks, it was Hanging Rock that brought fame to the area, largely through *Picnic at Hanging Rock*. The story became embedded in folklore as a possibly true, unsolved mystery, centred on the disturbing disappearance of schoolgirls at Hanging Rock on Valentine's Day, 1901.

Some amount of respectful fear is sensible in such a

place. The different layers of life and reality that emanate from certain natural structures are complex, potent, and fascinating. Hanging Rock was a place of ancient sacred beauty—far more than a place of sinister modern mystery. However, if it weren't for the story, it would still be relatively unknown, sitting quietly as it had for six million years, with a mere 26,000 years of First Nations people treading its ground.

Geboor, Hanging Rock, and the township of Black Forest made an energetic triangle. Maliyan sensed it and felt both safe and challenged within its confines. However, other triangles soon began to mysteriously appear.

CHAPTER 25

THE OAK TREE WIZARD

Every evening, before dark, Maliyan walked along the creek next to her house. As she loved being outside, the dusk walk was a last breath of nature before morning.

A few days before full moon, she noticed that one of the grand oak trees had strange arrangements around it. She stopped to investigate. On the first day, a large circle of leaves bordered the tree as if to mark some territory. Every consequent day, varying-sized piles of sticks were placed under the oak as if somebody was getting ready for a ceremony. To add to the mystery, an increasing number of triangles made from sticks appeared on the ground.

Maliyan became more and more convinced that it was the work of local witches preparing for the full moon.

They're probably called the Black Witches of Forest, she thought.

On full moon day, she decided to walk in a different direction.

The following evening, she returned to the oak and saw a senior man slowly getting out of his mobility machine. His right side was paralysed. With much deliberation, he pushed the leaves into a line around the oak and fiddled with the bundles of sticks. He looked nothing like a witch. In fact, he looked the epitome of conservativeness.

"What are you doing?" asked Maliyan.

Looking up startled, the man explained that he had worked in weed control and the best he could do now was confine himself to the weeds around this oak.

"I'm not against any plant," said the man, "but a weed is a plant in the wrong place."

He explained how he painstakingly pushed all the fallen leaves away from the trunk so he could spot the invasive weeds. Thus, the circle around the tree. He collected all the unwanted twigs into tied-up piles because, otherwise, he couldn't move them. Thus, the neat bundles.

"And the triangles?" asked Maliyan.

"Come look," he said, pointing to one with his stick. "The triangles mark the areas where suspected weeds are sprouting. To be sure, I must watch them for a while."

As the man seemed glad of the company, Maliyan told him how her little witch story had grown daily in her mind. He was not the sort of person to have ever contemplated witches. She figured he would tell himself that she was joking.

"I'm no witch," he laughed.

"Maybe a wizard?" said Maliyan with a wink.

"Maybe a weed wizard," smiled the man.

"The Oak Tree Wizard," said Maliyan with a bow, leaving him to his self-appointed task.

That serves me right for taking myself so seriously, thought Maliyan as she smiled and hurried along before the darkness set in. *I think I need a break from visiting Hanging Rock and Geboor. Tomorrow, I'll head out into the gentler pastures with content cows, rusty Utes with old-time farmers rattling along the bumpy roads, and impatient young men driving around the familiar bends at breakneck speed (because young men have always done that). But right now, I'll head home for dinner.*

PART III
IDOLS
WINTER

WEAVING DREAMS

CHAPTER 26

BLACKPOOL FEVER

In late May and early June, a sickness takes over the ballroom dancing world. A magic sort of sickness called Blackpool Fever. It doesn't matter if the dancer has been to Blackpool or not, if they aspire to go or don't, if they religiously watch every livestream or the occasional social media video. Since its inception a century ago, Blackpool Dance Festival has become the most prestigious international ballroom dancing competition of the year.

Champions have fought and been crowned on the hallowed grounds of the Empress Ballroom at the Winter Gardens, Blackpool, England. Fierce battles have been waged in that consecrated space of spectacular architecture. The grand ballroom carries the scars and spoils of war in the air.

Once victorious, those revered world champions have been even more fierce in defending their titles. They are the high-heeled, sparkly soldiers, the slicked-hair, perfectly tailored warriors, ticking bodies pitched to perfection with years of intense practice, learning, and finding their unique edge. Those finely-tuned, expensive bodies are driven by concentrated single-mindedness.

The champions forge the way for all dancers—young and old, talented and terrible, rich and poor, gracious and nasty. They blow wind into the sails of countless admiring dancers who reach for their own dancing betterment.

Beneath the champions are the troops of dancers who, somehow or other, make the annual pilgrimage to Blackpool despite financial, physical, emotional, and sometimes national difficulties. Each one contributes to the living mass of bodies and souls yearning for the satisfaction of a dance well-danced. A nod from teacher, a mark from respected judge, a smile from partner, applause from a stranger in the audience, a compliment from someone's mother, a glow from inside oneself.

CHAPTER 27

IDOL MAKER AND BREAKER

The thread of Geboor was not only sewing a garment in Maliyan's consciousness but also pulling apart some of the old stitching. In particular, it was picking out all the old idols.

Idols are both material and nonmaterial forms. They are anything that becomes a God to us. Not to break anyone's dreams, but spiritual seekers are not allowed idols. Not any. None. One by one, they get taken away. Sometimes, it's quick and deadly, but you have to be tough for that.

The breaking of idols is not a dream breaker. It is a fear breaker. Getting rid of them is not to create pain. It is to take away pain. The spiritual path doesn't annihilate the source of our happiness. It gives us the possibility of real happiness.

During Blackpool Fever, a certain type of unnamed fear put its hand on Maliyan's shoulder, and she couldn't shake it off. All her usual spiritual tactics didn't work.

One evening, she lay down to sleep, though sleep did not come easily. Her body was tired, but her mind would not settle. When she finally drifted off, it was shallow and uneasy.

She woke suddenly, straight into fear. It gripped her chest, then spread panic through her body. She could not move. It felt as though she were falling from a great height, but there was no ground to hit. At the same time, something inside her was being pulled out. She tried to hold herself together, but there was nothing to hold. She was coming apart.

There was no space for understanding. She called to her spiritual protectors. Not with words, but with a desperate reaching. In such moments, you do not choose who you call. You call by instinct.

Gradually, the intensity eased. Not gone, but less absolute. Enough for her to breathe, to lie there, still and awake, until morning came.

The next day, the fear had thinned but not disappeared. It sat in her like something unfinished. It had come at the height of Blackpool Fever. The idols she had made—and the ones she had taken on without knowing—were being undone.

Something important was being rebuilt in her. Something clean and white. Something that would leave no mark.

> The idol which deceives
> is an idol weaving dreams.
> It surely will delay
> the coming of the day.

Fall, it must,
for an idol is a lie.
The treasure it would seek
becomes the wind-borne dust.

Fear not its death,
a troubled tear,
a sleepless night,
the idol breaks apart.

But in the morning,
clean and white,
the idol leaves
no mark.

CHAPTER 28

ON THAT NOTE

There is an idol greater than Blackpool Fever, even for dancers. It is so ubiquitous, clever, and deeply submerged that almost everyone thinks it is their most cherished friend. It is the idol of the *special relationship*—the one people yearn for, suffer for, and yearn for again while never seeing its flawed nature. Rather than ensuring our love, the *special relationship idol* prevents us from truly loving others.

Fortunately, not all idols are broken abruptly and scarily. Most are broken very slowly, bit by bit, idea by idea, small suffering by small suffering. The spiritual path is kind and tender, rewarding its trekkers with obvious and valuable gains at every step.

The month in Black Forest had softened Maliyan's thoughts about Luna. She simply and gently forgot to be upset about anything to do with him. It no longer seemed to matter what he had done or might do or should do or shouldn't do.

And on that note, she started messaging him.

And he started messaging back.

BEYOND THE SOLSTICE

CHAPTER 29

COMMUTERS IN COMMON

"Are you off to work?" asked Maliyan as she crossed paths with her neighbour on her early morning walk.

"Yes," he said. "Can't miss the city train or I'll miss my train buddies."

"Long way to commute every day," said Maliyan.

"There are a lot of us who do," said the neighbour. "Many come from further out than here. We long-time country commuters have formed little groups over the years and know which carriage to get into. Some play cards. Some talk. There are football to philosophy groups and even a book club in one carriage. Some like their own company. They read, watch their phone, or stare out the window. We all like to do different things, but have one thing in common."

"What's that?" asked Maliyan.

"We know living in the country is worth the commute," he said. "We don't often say it, and even less so to city folk (in case they want to move here), but we all know why we are on that long ride. And not one of us would give it up for the world."

CHAPTER 30

SOLSTICE EPIPHANY

Two weeks ago in Nanima:

One advantage of owning a small business in the country is that the power is on the owner's side. In the city, that is not the case. You have to be on the ball and on your feet to keep your customers. In small country towns, there are not that many businesses. Often, there are gaping holes in what is available. The locals have to be grateful for the ones they've got because they can easily disappear and frequently do.

On that basis, Luna had a winter solstice epiphany. The winter solstice is the sun's rebirth. Instead of the days becoming shorter and darker, the tide turns, and they head in the opposite direction. Luna woke at 12.57 a.m. (the exact moment of change in the relationship between Earth and sun). He didn't know it was the winter solstice, but he knew what to do.

The next day, he put a sign on the front door of his cafe.

*In the interest of mental health, Luna Tiks
will have an extended winter break.
See you on the other side.*

A week later, Luna and Iggy set off on their solstice expedition. The plan was to stay in caravan parks that allowed dogs and slowly drive towards the northern sun. They first had to reach the Great Dividing Range. They would cross it, keep going to the city, and then turn left towards the northern coastline. However, when they arrived at the foot of the mountains, instead of ascending them, they turned right, southward.

In the same way that Luna listened to his solstice epiphany, he followed its driving directions. Perhaps not knowingly, not consciously, but he followed it, and that was all that really mattered. He told himself and Iggy that they could turn around at any point and head the other way. But they kept driving deeper into the southern countryside, keeping pace with the Great Dividing Range, and eventually moving into the Macedon Ranges.

CHAPTER 31

WINTER DEPTHS

In Black Forest:

Maliyan said goodbye to her commuting neighbour and headed for the coffee shop. She crossed the creek and momentarily watched its chilly, bubbling water.

One month of winter done, she thought.

Although most people long for the sunniness of early spring, she didn't want to wish the winter away because the dark times are as valuable as the light. It's a balance. It needs to be approached in the right way. Not wished away, not ignored, not merely endured with patience, but acknowledged and appreciated for what it was. In the dark soil, all life is born, including us as humans. Our bodies are made from the food we eat, and that comes from the soil. If the soil says it needs a rest, we should listen. Our bodies, likewise, have their own process of regenerating and reforming.

As Maliyan gave her coffee order (little more than coffee-flavoured hot milk), a large dog nuzzled her leg. She paid for her order and turned to see what the dog wanted.

It was an off-lead German shepherd. Big dogs have to be well-behaved to be off-lead. He seemed eager for a pat.

Strange for a German shepherd, thought Maliyan. *They tolerate pats from strangers. They don't actively seek them.*

A man laughed, and Maliyan looked up.

"I needed to escape the Nanima winter," said Luna.

"I think you've come deeper into it here," said Maliyan with surprised joy.

"Where are you staying?" she asked as she rested her hand on Iggy's strong, bony head.

"In the caravan park," said Luna.

Black Forest had a small caravan park, which struggled at the best of times, let alone in winter. Being too close to the city to be a holiday destination, Black Forest was a true country town. It didn't have the restless energy of visitors, except those who briefly stopped on their return from the nearby tourist attractions. It had the natural energy of people who lived, worked, and raised their families there. It had the settled nature of ordinary people going about their business, attending to their day, having their problems, having their victories, with time to smile at the people in the coffee shop queue, and with a willingness to help strangers who needed it.

"Has it got heating?" asked Maliyan.

"Yes," said Luna. "It's fine."

Winter-in-earnest wasn't the best time to arrive in Black Forest. Maliyan had the last part of autumn as her adjustment. Some things were already adjusted from when she moved from the city to Nanima, but Nanima was a different sort of country town to Black Forest. Although also cold in winter, Nanima had a dry, open, clear, earthy atmosphere. Black Forest was colder, wetter, foggier, and influenced by the proximity of Geboor and Hanging Rock, giving it a more intense, thick, pulsating energy.

In the first few weeks of living in Black Forest, Maliyan had an irresistible urge to drive in every direction and investigate every little town. One might say that it was animal instinct, and she was staking out her territory. We are part animal, and that part of us needs to function well. Otherwise, when we add the higher parts to our animal base, the latter will be stressed from the weight. The body is not a goal in itself, but it is the medium that makes it possible for us to be here.

Strangely, one morning, the desire to drive in all directions completely left her, and she settled into a more local routine with regular trips to specific places.

Arriving in Black Forest mid-winter is a bit of a jerking adjustment, thought Maliyan, *but it probably helps to reset the system.*

"It's all about the underwear," she said.

Luna looked confused.

"You know," explained Maliyan, "singlets, spencers, HeatTech, thermals—that sort of thing."

"Oh," said Luna.

"And go buy some flannelette sheets," suggested Maliyan.

"I won't be here long enough for that," said Luna.

Maliyan thought that whatever force brought Luna all the way from Nanima in the depths of winter would probably not be letting him go so easily.

THE MAN WHO KEPT
HIS DOORS OPEN

CHAPTER 32

FATHER DYLAN

Maliyan discovered an unexpected open door in a nearby town. One of the Catholic churches managed to keep itself unlocked while everyone else couldn't. A notice was stuck to the right-hand entrance door.

> *We especially welcome those who are single, married, divorced, widowed, straight, gay, questioning, well-heeled, or down-at-heel.*

It went on to include every other imaginable variant of human nature and circumstance. On the left-hand door was a recent letter from visitors. They explained that they came from another town and were of a different denomination. They had medical appointments nearby and were so pleased to sit quietly in the church afterwards.

On Maliyan's first visit, the church was beautifully empty. She walked around it slowly, gazing at the stained glass artwork, the statues, the candles, and the altar. She had no particular favouritism towards Catholicism. However, one shouldn't deny the lineage we come from. Dismissing one's religious heritage is as ignorant as dismissing one's ancestral heritage. It's in the DNA. Not just the physical DNA but the energetic, mental, and spiritual DNA.

Maliyan could enter any Catholic church and instantly access a vast storehouse of information from every part of the building. When she went into a church of another denomination, she could appreciate and understand many things, but there were other things she simply did not have access to on an energetic level. There was knowledge that was missing.

A stream of light bounced into the darkened church as the heavy front door was pushed open. Since her solitude was stolen, Maliyan watched the visitors and eventually wrote these words.

> So still.
> Nothing quite like it.
> The dense quiet in
> an old empty church.
>
> The thick stone walls
> keep the world out.
> The exquisite colour of
> stained glass lets it in.
>
> Not many come,
> though the doors
> are unlocked.
> Some do.

The Italian dad shows
his five-year-old
the water receptacle for
his baby sibling's baptism.

A man does not
want to say hello.
Maybe his wife died.
Maybe he is dying.

This is the place to come
for things like that.
Life and death do not escape
its thick stone walls.

The teenage girls
take photos below
the Virgin Mary.
They muffle their amusement.

It doesn't matter.
Life has the last
laugh on us all.
And churches catch it.

On her way out, she passed a wooden container with the painted words, *Poor Box*. The box was as old as the concept of calling community service something for *poor people*. She folded her poem, wrote a note on the back, and put it in the Poor Box.

Dear Father Dylan,

Thanks for keeping your church open. It's a pity when they aren't—a delight when they are.

Maliyan

CHAPTER 33

AIRPORT ARRIVALS

Father Dylan was as interested in meeting the woman who understood "the dense quiet" of his church as Maliyan was interested in meeting the man who kept his doors open. So, she went to Mass.

He was a round man. Round-headed, round-bellied, round in nature (no sharp edges), and possessing a full-bodied, round voice, which he used loud and proud for all the singing sections of Mass. He looked like he could have been one of the local sheep farmers as much as a priest. Not pious. Down-to-earth. He liked people and wanted them to like him. He still had plenty of the Irish lad in him who, he said, used to scour the paddock with his aunt's metal detector looking for lost Viking gold. He never found any but did find a few modern coins, which he suspected were planted by his aunt to keep him outside and away from her kitchen.

Being in his mid-fifties, he had been a priest for a long time. It meant he got through the challenging earlier years when the sexual drive of celibate priests has to get subli-mated with no viable help from the establishment. Some leave (or never join), some suffer in silence, some have affairs (and suffer a different sort of silence), some develop relationships with their same-sex co-priests (which may or may not have happened in different circumstances), and some, unfortunately, get sick and inflict their suffering on innocent children. Many struggle through it, but there are a few who have such a strong and intent devotion to their spiritual path that their physical drives get sorted through spiritual practices and they do not feel deprived by their life choices.

All that was behind him, and Father Dylan could concentrate on other matters, such as life. And death. His mother died in Ireland a few months back. He was the sort of man not ashamed of loving his mother or grieving her death.

"I have a story to tell you," said Father Dylan hesitantly in the sermon. "I don't want to sound away with the fairies, and I'm not sure if I believe in dreams."

There's nothing to believe or disbelieve about dreams, thought Maliyan. *They are a different level of awareness, ranging from ego ranting to dimensional doorways.*

"You will never guess who came out of the international airport arrivals door," said Father Dylan. "My mother! She said she couldn't tell me about Heaven but looked so happy. I now believe in Heaven more than ever."

There's nothing to believe or disbelieve about Heaven either, thought Maliyan. *Heaven is a state of consciousness. It speaks for itself.*

She was happy for Father Dylan and had a hunch that his mother played a part in bringing her to the doors of the man who kept them open.

TALKING TO THE MOON

CHAPTER 34

LOOKING FOR LOVE

When Luna was in Nanima, he didn't get much chance to be bored because he worked most days. However, in Black Forest, he had neither cafe to run, house to care for, nor town with things to do. Presumably, to avoid heading back north, he made lots of trips to the nearby city. If it didn't suit to take Iggy, he left him with Maliyan.

When Luna collected Iggy one afternoon, Maliyan said, "It's been a lovely sunny day here, and there's still a few hours of light left. Do you feel like coming with me to the top of Lying Lady?"

"Lying Lady?" questioned Luna.

"Geboor, Mount Macedon," said Maliyan. "Don't you see her on your way back from the city?"

"Ah, yes," said Luna. "When I drive over the outward-bound city bridge on the way home, I see her on the far left."

Encouraged by Luna calling Black Forest home, Maliyan ventured, "How are you liking it here?"

"It's not really my thing," said Luna.

As Maliyan reversed her car onto the street with Luna aboard, a neighbour from down the road approached and wanted to chat. Mostly, he wanted to know who Luna was. He was an older man, but not so old that he wasn't still looking for love.

Maliyan had made the mistake of responding warmly to him earlier on and then had a hell of a time getting rid of him. Not that she wanted to get rid of him exactly. He was a neighbour, after all. But if she gave him an inch, he took a mile.

He was a proper English gentleman, raised with money and good manners, but lacking relationship skills. There was nothing harmful about him, and his efforts at seducing would have been amusing if they weren't so darn annoying. With all his proclamations of being lonely and needing someone, he never once bothered to ask Maliyan about herself.

How stupid, thought Maliyan. *If you were interested in someone, wouldn't it be sensible to find out something about them? Before you even started, wouldn't you want to know if they were open to the idea rather than assuming they were single, lonely, and available for dating? Wouldn't it be wise to ask about the person's basic likes and how they spent their time rather than presuming they would be interested in you on the extremely broad basis of simply being a man?*

Although he had little inclination to ask questions or listen to anything told to him, he showed remarkable resilience in not giving up. Maliyan thought that if he put a fraction of his persistence into trying to communicate properly, he would be a transformed man with many friends and probably love interests. Instead, he got neither girlfriend nor friend out of his neighbour because he took every slight sign of friendship as a willingness to relieve his aloneness.

Luna looked at Maliyan oddly when she drove off a bit too quickly, leaving her neighbour (who seemed like a nice old man) staring after them.

CHAPTER 35

CAMEL'S HUMP

Instead of driving to the top of Geboor, Luna and Maliyan parked at Camel's Hump, the part of Lying Lady that looked like a pubic bone. They made the short climb to the lookout along with a few late-afternoon tourists.

"Why is it called Camel's Hump?" asked a ten-year-old boy. "I don't see any camels."

"You need some distance," said his Dad. "Then you can see the hump of the camel."

"Perspective makes all the difference," Maliyan said quietly to Luna.

"I thought it was called Camel's Hump, as in tight pants on a guy," whispered Luna. "Like male ballet dancers in tights."

"I think that would be a two-humped camel," said Maliyan. "This is a one-humped camel."

On the way down to the car park, Maliyan said, "You have a point about the hump."

"I do?" said Luna.

"When you see Lying Lady from far away, the pubic

bone bulge is too big for a female," said Maliyan. "Our lady must be part man. Anyway, Camel's Hump is made from the same stuff as Hanging Rock, and that is definitely male."

"It *is* called Camel's Hump," said Luna with a wink, "not Camel's Toe."

CHAPTER 36

NIL ILL-WILL

On the way back down the mountain, Luna asked Maliyan if she had found anywhere to dance yet.

"I've looked at two studios in nearby towns," said Maliyan.

One studio was a social one—full of people her age with low-level ability but enthusiastic attitude. The other studio was smaller but had better dancers—younger, more serious, better technique, and higher level teaching.

"I'm going to go to the young studio," said Maliyan. "It puts me in a position of constantly failing, but if I dance around people my age and ability, I'll stay the same."

"Better to be the worst house in the street than the best," offered Luna. "Not saying you are the worst..."

Maliyan laughed and said, "It's okay. I can handle it. Anyway, it's good for me. It's humbling."

"Will you do competitions again?" asked Luna.

"The thing I love about dancing is dancing," said Maliyan.

She loved her lessons. She loved practising. She didn't like competitions. Ultimately, it is the dancing that all dancers love—to be one with the body, another body, the music, the movement, and the spirit of life. Along the way, that love often gets distorted. But it is still there, waiting to be reignited.

"Competitions turn everyone into competitors," said Maliyan.

"Unsurprising," said Luna.

"Dancers view other dancers as enemies," said Maliyan. "Teachers eye each other off as threats. Adjudicators compete for pride of place. There are false idols everywhere."

"Don't do it then," said Luna.

"The thing I like about competing," said Maliyan, "is that you get to share your whole-hearted, best dancing efforts with people who would otherwise never see them. That has nil ill-will."

CHAPTER 37

PERFECT MISMATCH

As Luna got out of the car, he said, "It's sort of strange that you ended up in latin—all the makeup, the clothes (or lack of them), and the way of moving. It's not really your style."

"I'm more made for ballet than latin," said Maliyan, "but I guess the mismatch of it keeps me here."

> I'm made for ballet,
> not latin, but I'm
> latin enmeshed.
>
> I'm at home with the ethereal,
> not the earth-real, but I'm
> latin encaptured.
>
> More aligned with ballet lines.
> Fixed spine, moving limbs,
> no curves, no face.

In latin, curves are in
and body is out—
out and about on show.

Ballet bodies have neither
sexuality nor individuality.
Closed hips, closed lips.

Latin bodies are as
sensual as they are personal.
Open hips, open lips.

In ballet, one could
disappear into ethereal,
empty-faced egolessness.

Latin keeps you in
body-touching,
hand-searching,

hip-gyrating,
feet-earthing,
centre-rotating,

weight-moving,
face-opening
groundedness.

A constant battle
that cannot be won.
It keeps me here.
A perfect mismatch.

Luna kissed Maliyan goodbye and said, "Thanks for babysitting Iggy, and I'm glad something keeps you here."

PART IV

JOY

SPRING

CHANGING STATES

CHAPTER 38

SPRING RENEWAL

After his month-long retreat in the Nanima poustinia in early autumn, Francis decided to organise a 30-year spring reunion of the charismatic inner-city community he and Maliyan once belonged to, *Spirit of Joy*. That meant an interstate trip for Maliyan.

The Charismatic Renewal Movement comprises Christians who share the Pentecostal emphasis on healing and "gifts of the Spirit" but remain part of their mainstream churches. The movement is fundamentalist in doctrinal nature, thus the reason for its shortcomings and the abdication of many maturing members. Inequality of the sexes does not sit well with blossoming, talented, confident young women or, for that matter, their thinking male counterparts. Nevertheless, charismatic communities tend to be absolutely alive and full of genuine healing—a far cry from mainstream churches.

The Spirit of Joy community had a short but powerful prime of a few years. Those few years in that potent place of spiritual awakening deeply impacted all the participants. Many of the couples attending the reunion had found their spouse there. It was the sort of community that fostered intense commitment, faith, and hope. Pairing and marriage were a natural response.

When the Spirit of Joy disbanded, some of its members moved to a similar type of community in the city's outer western suburbs and had been there ever since. It was the most central place to have the reunion.

CHAPTER 39

JUST JOY

At the get-together, Maliyan looked around the group of white, grey, and hairdresser-coloured heads. All had large families, mostly grown now, five children being the average. Without exception, they were good people. Given the intense spiritual dedication required of the original Spirit of Joy members, it was impossible that this group could have lost its spiritual bent. Perhaps, here and there, some got lazy. Perhaps some grew slowly. Perhaps life got in the way at stages. But a fire like that can't be extinguished.

One particular man was unrecognisable to Maliyan. In his youth, he was tall and blonde with a fine, fit body from bike-riding long distances and other sporty things that young men like to do. He was quick to smile and slow to criticise. He came from a cultured, attentive family and had the privilege of a good education and the freedom to develop his creative talents. He chose a career in the creative arts. He was still tall and slim, but his blonde hair was white. Although other people's lined faces carried their original personalities, his did not.

Maliyan continued talking to him longer than others as she was searching for him. Several times, she thought she must have mistaken his identity. She kept making silly jokes to get him to laugh because his free-spirited, handsome smile was what she remembered most about him. Her jokes did not deserve a great response, but now and again, the familiar smile crept over his face and gave it a little light so that she knew it wasn't a case of mistaken identity at all.

What has happened to him? thought Maliyan as she tried to coax him out of his somewhat condescending seriousness. *This is a good man. Whatever has happened, it's not out of lack of conscientious duty. Duty, ah yes. That's the problem.*

Decades ago, he gave up his creative career for full-time work in the church. He had heavy responsibilities and, as often happens, had become guardian of right and wrong. As joy and humility go together, so do duty and self-importance. Not that he was arrogant. He was self-important in the humblest of ways. He would have considered himself to be a servant of the people. Nevertheless, he had divorced Joy and married Duty.

Maliyan made one last silly joke. The long-time friend looked at her quizzically and a little distrustingly.

And as they had done thirty years ago, they parted company.

CHAPTER 40

TRAINING IT

After the reunion, Francis dropped Maliyan at the nearby railway station. The reunion suburb was at the foot of the mountains that had to be crossed to reach Nanima. The train wasn't the fast, comfortable, clean express country train. It was the regular dirty, crowded suburban train that happened to go all the way to the other side of the mountains. A bus would connect for the rest of the trip. A five-hour journey altogether.

The train was full, as it had made many city stops before it got this far. Maliyan had to sit next to two couples in their early thirties who had been on an escape trip to the city without their young children. She knew all about them because their loud voices matched their inability to tastefully monitor their conversation. The youngest of the foursome, an attractive girl in her late twenties, kept looking out the window at each station and commenting on the arses of the men walking past.

They bitched for a good hour about some "friend" with five children. They each had two.

The arse-watching girl said, "The other day, she

fucking told me I should try for a girl and have a third kid."

She raised her volume and continued, "Why would I do that? I fucking hate kids!"

Delightful.

They stayed on the train until it descended the mountains. Fortunately, they didn't line up for the connecting bus. However, they had equally enjoyable (but less offensive) matches on the bus. Two older people talked loudly and incessantly on their mobile speakerphones to family members back home. Their long, tedious, meaningless conversations bounced around the bus until the hum of the road and the silence of the paddocks eventually got the better of them, and they hung up.

As the sun turned in for the night and gave its parting gift of glowing gold, the bus pulled into Nanima—a welcome sight.

HEART CENTRE

CHAPTER 41

HALF AN EYE

I n *Maliyan's Nanima garden:*
Spring in Nanima was a pleasant change to Black
Forest's wintery spring. The mornings were cold, but
the day cheerily bounced into a much sunnier mildness by
mid-morning.

"Thanks for helping me get my garden ready for selling
the house," Maliyan said to Luna, who had driven back to
Nanima when Maliyan flew to her reunion.

The townsfolk were happy to have Luna Tiks open
again and even more so to have their Luna back. They
genuinely missed him, although he said he didn't know
why. People generally cannot tell their impact on other
people. Only by observing how people react to us can we
usually know what we send out into the world.

Luna told Maliyan that he said all sorts of nice things
to customers (that he didn't mean) to keep them coming
back. Nevertheless, he did it with such enthusiasm that it
didn't matter whether he meant it or not.

It wouldn't take long to fix Maliyan's garden, as it
wasn't large. It was completely overgrown when she

bought the house two years ago. Underneath the weeds and rubbish were many surviving plants, relieved to see the light of day. They responded by growing profusely and prettily. Her winter absence had minimal impact on the garden. However, in the one month of spring since her return, the garden had run away with itself.

Under the large gum tree, next to some lavender bushes buzzing with bees, Maliyan turned to face Mount Arthur.

"I'll be back in ten minutes," she said. "I have something to do."

Sitting down, she crossed her legs, closed her eyes, and became as still as a statue. Luna stared at her motionless body and remembered that he told her she was on the spectrum when she was staying in his shophouse at the beginning of the year. It made him smile. Not everything that happened this year made him smile, but that did. He didn't know why she was the way she was. Was she on the spectrum? Could she see a different world from others? Was it the same thing? Would it be a good thing if more people saw things differently?

He walked towards her and then stopped. He felt it was a place he didn't belong. It wasn't that he was unwelcome. It was his choice. He didn't want to go there. He carried on gardening and kept half an eye on her vacant body.

CHAPTER 42

MINDLESS MAGIC AND MINDFUL MEDITATION

Maliyan's spirit body removed itself from her physical body. It lifted off the ground and slowly rose higher. Being midday in early October, the temperature was a pleasant 22 °C. The breeze was gentle and cleansing. In the yogic tradition, it is called a wind bath. It is as therapeutic as a water, mud, or fire bath. A bath or shower at the end of the day eliminates a million tempers and calms as many worries. Mud baths are for health and healing, as every young child knows when they make a beeline for puddles to squelch through and mud patches to make pies. Fire baths for the aura are energetically purifying.

At 200 feet, Maliyan scanned the township below. The remains of the low-lying bridge, half washed away in the floods last year, stood pathetically at the intersection of the Bell and Wambul Rivers. It hadn't been repaired. Many things in the country have to wait a long time before limited financial resources get sent their way.

Further downstream was a large group of grazing kangaroos. It reminded Maliyan of the intuitive ways farmers read the weather. The ending of a long, dry spell was of particular importance.

Some farmers believed that an unusually large number of kangaroos by the river at daybreak signified coming rain. One old-timer swore by his trumpet. He said that rain was not far away if he got three echoes from playing a particular note. Some said echidnas making their way uphill indicated significant rainfall.

There was probably truth in all of it, as these were people of the land. They lived and worked with it, befriended and understood it. In the hands of city dwellers, their curious weather forecasting methods would be no more than mindless magic.

Maliyan's gaze followed the postman on his pushbike, methodically moving around the streets of Nanima. He yelled out greetings as he went. He was too far away for her to hear, but she knew the sorts of things he said.

Gotta watch out for those buggars of magpies. The trick is to get the mothers used to you before the babies are born. Then they won't swoop 'cause they know ya.

Got me travelling wardrobe for this time of year. When I started this mornin', it was bloody freezin'. Won't be long and it'll be stinkin' hot.

Just beyond the postman was Euroka's hut on the Bell. He was the reason for her travels. When he returned from Uluru at the end of last year, reclaiming his hut (precipitating Maliyan's stay in Luna's shophouse), he told Maliyan that the purpose of travelling to the Red Centre had been accomplished. He originally said he was going there to die. As he returned alive, Maliyan did not know what had happened, and he never spoke about it.

Although Maliyan rarely saw him, Euroka's journey stayed in her mind as one that was also hers. She had neither money nor time to travel to the desert, especially as her current focus was on selling her house and permanently moving to Black Forest. Yet, something told her she must go to Uluru before leaving Nanima.

It was only in her garden today that she suddenly knew how. She also knew Luna would watch over her body while she was gone. He would not question her about it because, frankly, he wouldn't want to know.

CHAPTER 43

MIGHTY MONOLITH

Someone was sitting on the riverbank in front of Euroka's hut. Maliyan assumed it was Euroka. However, on closer inspection, it was Bell-Bell. She was excited to have Maliyan back in Nanima and equally upset when told that her return was temporary. Bell-Bell's spirit body rose from her motionless physical body and moved towards Maliyan. She sent a wordless request to accompany Maliyan on her journey. Maliyan communicated that she could but needed to remain silent.

The speed of their movement upwards substantially increased until they reached 5,000 feet, a height at which many small planes fly. They moved horizontally at a further increased pace until a red spot appeared on the horizon. As they drew closer to the spot, it grew in size, majesty, and presence to become the world's largest single rock structure: Uluru. To add to its glory, what is seen is only a fraction of its totality. It is a mostly buried marvel in the vastness of the desert, which extends endlessly in every direction.

The women descended from 5,000 to 1,000 feet and

landed on top of Uluru. At 30 °C, the temperature was hotter than Nanima's but still comfortable. This was the last month before the long stretch of desert heat set in.

In 1985, the whole region was handed back to the Aboriginal people. However, it was only in 2019 that the tourist climb to the top of Uluru was finally banned. It had been requested many times that tourists not climb the rock, as that was for initiated Aboriginal men. It was a sacred site, not to be trampled or disrespected. Maliyan knew this powerful portal of energy was for men's business, but she came as neither female nor male, white nor black. She came as a spirit, ancient as the rock. It did not escape her that if she had physically travelled to Uluru, she would not have been able to get to the top. She and Bell-Bell could see the tourists at the bottom of the monolith doing the six-mile base walk.

Bell-Bell looked at Maliyan with an expression that said, *What now?*

We wait.

They waited until the sun disappeared at 7 p.m. and turned everything into a spectacular fireball of spitting energy. Red is a stimulant—of the body and all the energy systems. It is the colour of fire. Without fire, we cannot create anything. It is the colour of blood. Without blood, we shrivel and die. It is the colour of heart. Without heart, we destroy everything. It is the colour of Uluru, the fiery iceberg, the spiritual heart of the continent.

Long before white people and even before black people, this rock of red came from the earth. It raised its head and then patiently sat. It sat for a long time but was not bored. You can only be bored when you know minutes and hours. When you know eons, time disappears.

It was still waiting when the first people came to the

area 30,000 years ago—black people. It was waiting when the first white man laid eyes on it in 1873. White people came with all their ideas, terrific and terrifying, and with all their renaming of things that already were known, named, and loved. This red place was waiting for Maliyan and Bell-Bell. It will go on waiting for you. And when you and I are gone, it will still be waiting.

When you are half a billion years old, what is a human lifetime or two? Uluru is a mindful meditator who has forgotten to count time or anything.

CHAPTER 44

RED ROOT AND
DANGEROUS DOGS

R ed is also the colour of the root chakra at the base of the spine. It is your connection to tribal survival and belongingness in the world. Maliyan took the red of the sunset, the red of the desert sand, the red of the sandstone monolith, and the red of her foundational life force and held it in her being.

An hour after sunset, the Milky Way turned its lights to full beam. It pranced across the black backdrop, becoming more entrancing and theatrical as it went. The stars were incomprehensible in number and age. They gave direction to those moving through the dark terrain. They were a reminder that all was well, no matter what may be happening. For many cultures, they were the celestial river one must cross at death.

Maliyan averted her subtle-eyes from the sky as she heard a faint sound nearby. It was a snake on the hunt. Sensing the women, it turned toward them and slid down the rock surface. Maliyan indicated to Bell-Bell that they should follow. The park was closed, so no one was around.

Not tourists, anyway. They followed the snake to the base of the rock. It paused at the edge of a still rock pool, turned towards them again to entice them onwards, and slid into the water of Mutitjulu Waterhole.

The waterhole was as sacred as Uluru. In the semi-arid environment of limited, precious water, it provided physical and spiritual life. Like the river of Milky Way stars, it was an energetic passageway. As an Aboriginal person, Euroka would have had access to the waterhole through the Mutitjulu Community, Uluru's caretakers, who live within the park.

An aggressive, transparent dingo appeared at the water's edge and growled at them menacingly. He meant business and meant for them to leave.

"We'd better move away," said Bell-Bell.

"No, it's okay," said Maliyan. "The subtle spirits are gentle creatures. They use the ferocity of the dingo to guard the waterhole because they don't have that type of energy in them, like gentle people with guard dogs. We must convince him that we are worthy of entering the waterhole."

Calling the dingo a dog gave Bell-Bell an idea.

"I know what to do," she said enthusiastically. "I *love* dogs."

"Ahh, I don't think he'll like that sort of..."

Too late. Bell-Bell approached the dingo with bubbling affection. The dingo took offence and lunged at her. It was rather comedic, and Maliyan couldn't help laughing. However, for good measure, the dingo bit Bell-Bell on the arm. The women retreated behind a rock for safety.

"Are you alright?" asked Maliyan.

"Yes," said Bell-Bell. "I can't feel anything."

"I hope it stays that way," said Maliyan with concern. "Stay here. If I'm not back by daybreak, return to Nanima alone."

CHAPTER 45

SUBTLE SHELL

A message came from the ancient monolith. *Make your outer shell so thin that the dingo will not know you are there.*

Maliyan understood that when the outer shell was solid, the dingo would smell you and chase you away. You would bounce back to Earth.

Tread lightly, she thought. *Think not of dingo or yourself. Think of dissolution—a tiny point in the endless vastness of desert and night sky.*

The dingo sat quietly, head on paws, next to Mutitjulu Waterhole as Maliyan entered the water. She saw the snake that led them from the top of Uluru and many others beside.

How do I get through all the snakes to the other side of the waterhole? thought Maliyan.

The outer shell is thin, said the ancient monolith. *Let the inner one melt.*

At that point, Maliyan felt there were three options: to become afraid and be attacked by the snakes; to dissolve entirely and disappear into the eternal, etheric Milky Way;

or to dissolve just enough to pass through them and regroup on the other side.

She chose the third option. She sensed that if she made it to the other side, she could consciously incarnate wherever she wanted, rather than unconsciously bouncing back via the growling dingo. Probably that is what Euroka did. Thus his return to Nanima.

Maliyan could remember no more. She did not know what had happened in the water. Nor could she remember what it was like on the other side of the waterhole, if she made it. The next thing she knew, she was back in her body and in her garden. She wondered how much time had passed. The sun was high, so it must have only been minutes. She hoped Bell-Bell also got back safely.

Luna had not noticed her return. He was weeding the rose patch and telling one of the struggling bushes how good it was looking. Maliyan thought that he really needed a garden for his health and well-being. The shophouse didn't have one.

"I'm back," said Maliyan.

Luna didn't bother replying to that because, clearly, she had been sitting under the gum tree beside the buzzing lavender bush all along.

COSY AND CONSCIOUS

CHAPTER 46

COSY

The Wambul made its watery way down the Great Dividing Range, flowed through the foothills and slopes to get to Nanima, and wound further west to Thubbo, past the rural airport.

Country airports are so agreeable compared to city ones. The staff are relatively unstressed and genuinely friendly. The thirty-seat, twin-engine propeller plane usually took off with fewer than ten people. Everyone could stretch out, no one was breathing on anyone, and the air hostess was happy to chat and give out cups of tea and biscuits. It was bumpier than a jet plane because you fly lower, and the weather has a greater impact. However, Maliyan told herself that the pilots and air hostesses had done the route many times and always got back to their families. The lower altitude also meant a captivating view of the countryside. The day-long, tiring drive from Nanima to Black Forest was transformed into a one-hour, relaxing, fascinating ride.

Although there was plenty of room in the plane, Maliyan did have someone sitting next to her. It was Bell-

Bell. The day after returning from Uluru, Bell-Bell's father died. She was coming to Black Forest for his funeral and to sell his house, which Maliyan had been using over the winter. It was the first time they had talked since their Red Centre journey (other than arranging flight tickets). Maliyan did not know if Bell-Bell remembered any of the adventure. It turned out she didn't.

"I must have known my father was going to leave," said Bell-Bell, "because, for no apparent reason, I woke up with a sore arm the day he died."

"Is it getting better?" asked Maliyan.

"No," said Bell-Bell.

"There's our Lying Lady," said Maliyan, pointing to Geboor as the cosy little plane circled and started to descend.

CHAPTER 47

CONSCIOUS CHOICE

The two women spent the next few weeks getting Bell-Bell's father's house ready for sale. Although Maliyan had made it clean and functional, the garage, garden shed, kitchen and linen cupboards, and spare room were full of possessions. Mostly junk.

"Thanks for helping me," said Bell-Bell. "It's much nicer than doing it on my own."

Maliyan shrugged as if to say it was the least she could do after staying there so long.

"It's therapeutic," continued Bell-Bell. "I'm working through lots of memories as I go."

"What about the old push mower?" asked Maliyan. "Do you want to keep it?"

"Did you use it?" asked Bell-Bell.

"Sure did," said Maliyan. "I think the blades are a bit blunt, but it's good exercise having to push it back and forth over the grass."

Many things that senior folk did as part of life (and which are now considered old-fashioned, inconvenient, or inefficient) had a practical, environmentally friendly, and life-sustaining reason behind them.

Manual lawnmowers were noiseless, beneficial for health, and didn't need fuel. Outside washing lines were the norm, and dryers were reserved for incessant inclement weather. Before dryers, a hanging rack worked just fine. Heating was not wasted on whole houses. Doors were closed for unused rooms, and door snakes were used to keep out drafts. Bedding was changed to be seasonally appropriate, so artificial heat was unnecessary. Prepared food was rarely bought. Fresh, simple, basic but nutritious food (often grown locally) was cooked every day. A daily walk to the shops was the norm. Only what was needed and could be carried home was bought.

To be fair to modern folk, our older people didn't usually do all these things out of environmental consciousness. They did it because they didn't have a choice.

We do have a choice, and whatever it is, it should be conscious.

CHAPTER 48

GRACE OF GEBOOR

"If you stay here in the house with me," said Bell-Bell, early one afternoon, "I won't sell it. I'll move from Nanima to Black Forest."

"I can't do that, darling," said Maliyan.

"I didn't think so," said Bell-Bell a little dejectedly.

"You could move here anyway," said Maliyan gently. "How is your arm?"

"About the same," said Bell-Bell. "It still hurts."

"Why don't you have the rest of the afternoon off," suggested Maliyan. "I'll finish preparing the house for the real estate photographers. You go to Geboor."

"You don't want to come?" asked Bell-Bell.

"You'll get more from her on your own," said Maliyan.

LATER THAT DAY:

"The wind up there is still brisk," said a rejuvenated Bell-Bell on her return from Geboor.

"It takes a while for spring to hit," said Maliyan.

"When looking down on Black Forest," said Bell-Bell, "I thought about all the things that were making me feel less than happy, starting with my sore arm. As my breathing settled, the mountain began to take hold of my mind. I remembered the poem Francis read us in the Nanima poustinia about taking the thread that was specifically ours and turning it into a garment so that we would breathe our existence with ease."

"Did you find your thread?" asked Maliyan.

"It's much thinner than I would have expected," said Bell-Bell, "and more transparent. It's much less *me* than I imagined, but yes, I did. I know it's mine because..."

She lifted her arm and announced, "My arm is better."

Walking to the table, she picked up the real estate information and dramatically threw it in the bin with her recovered arm.

"I feel lighter and brighter," said Bell-Bell. "I feel nurtured. The grace of Geboor is holding me."

"Don't get too comfortable," said Maliyan with a smile. "It doesn't just hold you. It eats you up."

CHAPTER 49

ALL I GOT

TEXT MESSAGE FROM LUNA

I've decided to sell Luna Tiks.

MALIYAN

Really? Have you had enough of your tree change? Are you moving back to the city?

LUNA

Yes. Sort of. And not exactly.

MALIYAN

You don't want to buy my house then?

LUNA

No, my love, although I'd love the garden.

MALIYAN

Do you miss the city?

LUNA

I miss some things about it.

LUNA

I miss you more.

MALIYAN

Miss you too.

LUNA

I took a risk moving to Nanima. I can do it again.

LUNA

I'm coming your way. I'll travel to the city for work.

LUNA

That's all I got.

Being born is the greatest risk of all. We're not sure how life will work out. But we're here, and we have to try. Otherwise, the Mutitjulu dingo and all the other karmic forces will send us rebounding back to Earth with no more consciousness than when we did our last round.

We need to learn how to make our living, our dying, and our returning to Earth an entirely conscious, loving, safe, and cosy process.

The End

SUMMARY OF NANIMA SERIES

A contemplative journey of spiritual evolution, soulful relationships, and the quiet healing power of nature.

Spanning four deeply personal and spiritually rich books—Nanima, Geboor, Sonder, and The Flat—this series follows Maliyan, an insightful and grounded seeker whose path unfolds across the quiet towns and wild landscapes of rural Australia.

Through shifting relationships, ancestral stirrings, and encounters with both seen and unseen guides, Maliyan's life becomes a mirror for our own inner transformation. Alongside her are Luna—intuitive, witty, and playfully avoidant as he learns to love truly—and Bell-Bell, whose brilliance and volatility reflect the challenges of change and the yearning for wholeness.

The *Nanima Series* offers not just a story, but a spiritual companion. It invites you to walk the path of growth gently, to listen deeply to the land and your own spirit, and to remember that evolution is both quiet and profound.

ABOUT THE AUTHOR

In Wellington, Australia, the rural town on which Nanima is based.

Donna Goddard is a spiritual author whose work blends clarity, devotion, and metaphysical insight. With more than twenty published books across spiritual nonfiction, fiction, poetry, and children's literature, she writes to uplift consciousness and offer healing through words.

Donna's Facebook author page has over 400,000 followers worldwide, and her YouTube channel has received 4 million views. Her books are read by spiritual seekers globally and are known for their honesty, poetic style, and transformative energy.

Her writing is an offering—to help others awaken their own inner spirit, trust its guidance, and create a life of depth, beauty, and quiet joy.

All links at https://linktr.ee/donnagoddard

RATINGS AND REVIEWS

Donna would be grateful for any ratings or reviews.

ALSO BY DONNA GODDARD

Fiction

Waldmeer Series: A Spiritual Fiction Series
Nanima Series: Spiritual Fiction
Enanika Series: Visionary Fiction
Riverland Series (children's fiction 6 to 9 years)
Foxie (children's fiction 7 to 12 years)

Nonfiction

Love and Devotion Series
Sweet Spirit Series
Consciousness Series
Meditation Series
Poetry Series
Love's Longing
Dance: A Spiritual Affair
Writing: A Spiritual Voice